Two Shadowed Hearts

Taila Cantrell

Contents

Dedication

To the women who need to be more than the box that they were stuffed into. Spread your wings and fly.
But it's okay to get "stuffed" sometimes too.

Trigger Warnings

Stalking

Kidnapping

MFM

DP

Mommy/Daddy Kink (titles only)

Mention of Past Abuse

BDSM. Keep in mind that this is a work of fiction. If you are interested in practicing BDSM, please do your research and be safe.

One

I knew I was being stalked. My shadows were restless, and the hairs on the back of my neck had been standing at attention for days. I was on edge; prey caught in a trap waiting for the predator to arrive. Even Bambi's overly perky mood and a hot black coffee wasn't improving my mood. I'd barely slept the last three nights, I could feel the shadowy magic hunting for me. I just couldn't figure out why they hadn't grabbed me yet. Three years was a long time to hunt someone. I knew their patience was going to run out any day now.

"Are you okay, Ris?" Bambi asked, concern showing in her grey eyes.

"Just not sleeping too well, Bams. I'll be okay." I waved her off, hoping she wouldn't push further. Bambi Cruor was a kind person. She cared deeply for the people around her. It would make her an amazing Priestess. With Fang by her side, the Blood coven would rise to a whole new level of power. The thought brought a small smile to my lips. My friend deserved her witch bond more than anyone I'd ever known. I wasn't sure I ever wanted to find mine, couldn't imagine dragging anyone into the fucked up life I had chosen for myself.

"Are you planning to come to the coven meeting tonight?" She asked. I cursed under my breath. Her grandmother had called me last week. My time as a refugee witch was coming to an end. I needed to either join the Blood Coven or move on from my life here. I expected Eileen was preparing the coven for Bambi to take over. She knew how close we were, not forcing Bambi to give me that ultimatum was a kindness. Just because I understood didn't mean it didn't hurt. Before I could think of a response, my phone rang.

"Larissa." I answered.

"My my, it's not often my daughter actually answers my calls." Papa's booming voice floated through the phone, "What do I owe the pleasure to today?"

"A lack of sleep." I groaned into the phone, "What do you want Papa? Is Gramma okay?"

"We're all still broken hearted, cher. I wish you'd come on home. If you'd just consider— "

I'd heard this lecture a million times, "Papa no. I'm not coming back until my conditions are met."

"They're unreasonable!" He shouted into the phone. Papa was right of course, that was the whole point of the conditions. The Priests of Shadow would never bend to the will of a young woman. Much less one that had left them high and dry like I had.

I hung up, slamming my phone down on the table, "Couyon." I met Bambi's concerned eyes, "I'm going to head home, afraid I'm not good company right now. I'll probably skip the coven meeting tonight. Get some sleep."

"You know if you need something all you have to do is ask." She responded, pulling me into a hug before I could escape the coffee shop.

"I know and I love you for it." I muttered, patting her back gently. I nearly ran from the shop, giving Fang a nod when I passed him. He had taken up a table outside, giving us privacy but he always made sure to keep Bambi in sight. I was glad she had someone like that. I turned the corner but watched as she nearly leapt into Fang's arms when she came out. I couldn't hear what she told him as they started walking in the opposite direction, but the furrow in his brows made me suspect it had to do with me.

I walked home slowly, letting my shadows scout ahead of me. When nothing seemed amiss I entered my small apartment. I locked all three deadbolts and closed the latch, ensuring no one could enter without making a lot of noise. The weariness in my bones forced me to sit down on my purple velvet couch. I had hunted for one for months, before happening across this one at a yard sale. It was my most prized possession. I sank in deeper, letting my head fall back and my eyes drift shut for just a few moments.

My eyes slammed open but saw nothing, my lungs struggled to find air. I flailed as shadows coalesced around me in a cacophony of chaos. I pulled them toward me, humming as they twisted and writhed away from me. I felt around until I found a light switch. The moment I flicked it on, most of the shadows went still, fading back into my skin. A few stayed near my balcony window, drawing my attention. I approached slowly, reaching for those shadows that immediately skittered away, sliding under the door and outside. A shiver ran up my spine, the feeling of being watched increasing a hundred-fold. I didn't allow myself to hesitate as I swung open the balcony door and stepped out into the crisp November air. I wasn't prepared for the hulking figure standing on my balcony to stumble backwards, nearly tumbling over the side. On instinct my shadows reacted, keeping the trespasser steady.

The man stood well over a foot taller than my five-foot frame. His hair was jet black, curling around his forehead in a way that I did not want to call cute. Black tattoos spiraled down his exposed arms mimicking shadows. Before he could speak, I pushed my shadows to wrap around his throat, pushing him down on his knees. "I don't know who you are, but I need a good reason not to throw you off this balcony."

"Be a real waste since you just saved my life." He choked out in a voice made of steel. "Squeeze harder, mommy. I'm sure you can do better than this."

My eyes widened, and I took a step back, "Who are you?"

"I am Alok LeGrand, and you are Larissa De Valois, the next Priestess of the Shadow coven and my future bride." He spoke as if my shadows weren't still squeezing around his neck.

"Well Mister LeGrand, you must not have gotten the memo. I left the Shadow Coven." I said, putting my hands on my hips.

He laughed, "Sure I've been told that, but I think you'll find a good reason to come back."

I knew I shouldn't play along with this conversation, but if this man had been stalking me for days maybe I could convince him to leave, "What is that?"

"Me." He grinned, his bright white teeth flashing in the dark.

I snorted, "Definitely not. Goodbye." I let my shadows flood back into my skin, empowering me as I used them to disappear.

I muttered a spell the moment I reappeared in my bedroom, ensuring no one could enter my home. I made sure every curtain was closed as well. I needed time to think and plan. Alok LeGrand had just solidified my plan. It was time to flee further north.

Two

I had forced myself to lay down and get a few more hours of fitful sleep, but the moment the sun was peeking through my bedroom window, I was up and ready. I pulled my bug out bags out of my closet, double checking that they had all my important documents. I threw in a few clothing items that I had collected since moving in here. It took an hour for my apartment to be clear of all of my personal effects. I threw the bags over my shoulders, taking a deep breath as I stared at my couch. I couldn't take it with me, even magic wouldn't let me figure out an easy way to tote it with me in my little sports car. I sighed, sitting my bags down again. I found a paper and pen and jotted a quick and hopefully vague note. I knew Bambi would come looking for me when she didn't hear from me in a couple of days. She couldn't try to find me. If she could, any witch or warlock could. At least she would take good care of my couch and the few other sparse items I'd decided to leave behind.

I finally forced myself to grab my bags and leave. I didn't want to. This tiny apartment had been home for two and a half years. The idea of going on the run again made my stomach clinch. I was tired of living in fear, but I just couldn't return to my coven. I couldn't give up my life and freedom. I knew all that they would take from me, and I couldn't let that happen. I couldn't end up exactly like my mother. She wouldn't have wanted me to.

My car sat in its usual spot; it's shiny pink paint dulled by the storm clouds rolling in. At least the weather would match my mood. I threw my bags in the trunk, before climbing into the driver's seat. I glanced down to find one of my shadows caressing a sliver of exposed skin. I petted it in the same way most people would pet a cat. I couldn't remember how long the shadows had been with me. They had manifested when I was too small to understand that they were my magic embodied. My shadows had been my protectors and my friends when everything had fallen apart. Even now, when I was miserable, they could bring a smile to my face. I don't know why the Mother and Father blessed me with them, but I would never take my shadows for granted.

I took a deep breath, throwing my car into reverse and forcing myself not to look back as I drove out of town.

I'd been driving for hours. The rain pounding down on my window had at least helped to keep me awake as I crossed states lines into Tennessee. I didn't know exactly where I was headed, but clearly, I had to get further away from home. North seemed like the best choice, maybe I would settle somewhere cold and dark. My shadows would love that. A part of me rebelled at the idea of continuing to run, but I wasn't ready to face the demons I'd left behind. Maybe if I got far enough away, they'd forget about me, move on, and I could create a new life somewhere else. Leaving Bambi behind hurt, but she had Fang now. She would be okay. Someday I would see my best friend again, I was sure of that.

The blue flashing light of a small diner caught my attention, and I decided to pull in. My stomach growled as I rushed inside, rain dripping off my jacket. The diner was small, with checkered black and white tile. It was decorated with various old albums, a dusty jukebox playing an old song I didn't recognize was the only noise to be heard.

"Welcome in, stranger. What can I get started for ya?" An old man asked from behind a counter.

"What's the cook's specialty?" I asked, taking a seat across from him.

"Makes the best burger in the whole state, and our onion rings are famous around these parts." He said, "Name's Heath by the way."

"Sounds delicious, Heath. Can I also get a black coffee?" I asked.

"I'll brew you up a fresh pot." Heath responded, before shouting my order into the back. "What brings you to our little town?"

"I'm just passing through." I responded, picking at lint on my pants.

"Bad time to be traveling alone young lady. That storm's only going to get worse. There's a decent motel about a mile up the road. My cousin is the night manager. I can call and have him hold a room for ya. If you'd like."

I smiled at his concern; it wasn't often I came across such a pure soul. "I'd certainly appreciate that, Heath."

"I'd be happy to. Wouldn't want my granddaughter traveling in a storm like this." He sat a cup down in front of me, before pulling out an old flip phone and walking to the back.

Even though I was alone the feeling of being watched suddenly invaded my senses. I ground my teeth, glancing out the dark window to see if I saw Alok watching. It didn't make sense to me why the Priests would have sent him to get me. He wasn't part of the coven when I'd left three years ago, and they didn't trust easily. That meant that something about Alok was special. I hoped I never found out what. The glass of the window was covered in raindrops, reflecting my face back to me. There was nothing out there except rain, but the feeling of being watched didn't ease as Heath sat my food down in front of me.

"My cousin has a room all ready for you. Just stop by the front desk and let them know you need your key." He said, "It's on the house, so don't you worry about paying for it."

"You didn't need to do that." I chastised him. I had plenty of money saved, I could have easily paid for a motel stay for a single night.

"It's the right thing to do ma'am. Didn't hurt my pockets at all." He responded.

I decided not to argue, instead digging into the food in front of me. "Okay, I see why this is the best burger around." I wasn't much of a burger person, but this was definitely in the top three I'd ever had. The juice dripped down my chin as I took another big bite. Cheesy goodness flooded my mouth causing me to moan.

Heath grinned, "You'll just have to come back and see me again sometime."

"I just might." I smiled back. It would be nice to settle down in a small town like this again, but I knew I was still too close to home. I ate in silence, savoring every bite of the hot, greasy food. "I better be getting out of here. I need some sleep before I hit the road again."

"Come by in the morning for some breakfast. My wife will be in running the place, but I'll let her know to expect you..." He paused, obviously waiting for something.

"Oh, I'm sorry. Rissa." I gave him my nickname. It was unlikely anyone would stop here looking for me, but just in case I didn't want to be easily traceable.

"Have a good night's rest, Rissa." Heath said, waving me. I ran back to my car, sliding into the driver's seat completely soaked. The rain had only gotten worse while I ate.

I creeped down the road, finding the sign for the motel after just a mile or so. I parked my car, choosing to leave my bags behind until morning.

"Hi, um. Heath said you'd have a room key for me." I said as I approached the desk. A sleepy looking, lanky man glanced up at me, extending his hand to give me a room key. "Room sixty-six."

"Thanks." I said, taking the key and rushing away. The feeling of being watched chased me all the way into the large bed. I stripped out of my wet clothes and tucked myself under the covers immediately. It didn't take long for me to drift off to sleep, the rain pelting the windows a relaxing symphony.

The feeling of hands lifting me drew me out of my deep sleep. I tried to flail but I was wrapped tightly in the blanket I'd been sleeping under. I could feel the magic that helped to keep me immobile.

"Sorry about this, cher, but I don't see another way to get you to come with us." I immediately recognized Alok's deep voice.

"Kidnapping is the only way?" I asked. My heart was beating out of my chest. I had no way out of this situation. I reached for my shadows wondering why they hadn't awoken me when I was in danger, only to find they didn't respond.

"In some cultures, kidnapping your future bride is an honor." He shot back. "Now go back to sleep. You won't want to be awake for the journey home."

"I don't want to go back to the Shadow coven." I whimpered. I was truly helpless as he carried me out of the motel. No one turned an eye toward us as he exited.

"Too bad, little Priestess." This voice caused a shiver to run up my spine. Sihr was here. A man I'd once loved, had promised to stay by his side. I had betrayed him, and now I was at his mercy. "Your little game is over."

Before I could respond, blackness overtook my mind, and I fell back into a dreamless sleep.

Three

My head pounded as I came awake, panic clawing at my throat. I sat up, glancing around the unfamiliar space. The room was huge, the bed I was laid on was possibly the biggest I'd ever seen, surrounded by black curtains. I reached for my shadows; the moment I touched my magic they appeared all around me. Most of them slumbered peacefully, but a few floated around the edges of the room clearly keeping watch.

"Looks like we're in real trouble now." I muttered, forcing myself to stand. I walked to the window, a bit of sunlight was trickled through the blinds, so I pushed them out of the way. I gasped when I looked out over the bayou. I hadn't seen the sight of my home in three years. A tear ran down my face, I only wished I was seeing it willingly. The swamps of Louisiana called to my very soul; I'd been raised out on the bayou. The memories of sitting on the boat with my mother as a young girl caused more tears to roll down my face. I needed to find Alok and Sihr before they informed the Priests I was back. I knew they hadn't yet, otherwise I'd already be in the coven circle being bound to them. I beelined for the door, only to find myself locked in this extravagant room. I pounded on the door, "Hey, let me out of here!"

I heard footsteps approach, so I moved out of the way, grabbing a vase by the door. I hid just in time for the door to swing open. Alok stood there looking confused, but only for a moment because

I launched myself at him, smacking the vase on his shoulder hard. It shattered, causing glass to cut into my hand. I hissed dropping the shards of glass as cut opened up across my palms. I'd been aiming for his head, but he was even taller than I remembered.

"Ow, that hurt." He snapped, grabbing both of my wrists in one of his large hands. "That is not how I expect guests in my home to behave."

"Are many of the guests in your home unwilling captives?" I snapped back.

He didn't respond, dragging me into the bathroom. He turned the sink on. I watched in silence as he got it to a comfortable temperature before carefully washing the blood from my hands. Once the water ran clear, he grabbed a plush towel, wrapping my injured hand up. He led me back into the bedroom, sitting down on the bed with me before he finally spoke. "Listen, Larissa I understand that we don't know one another, but I need you to be open with me. Why did you leave the Shadow coven three years ago?"

I chewed on the inside of my cheek, taken aback by his kind demeanor and strange line of questioning. "Sihr hasn't told you?" I asked, dodging this question.

"I don't want to hear his side of the story. I want to hear yours." Alok insisted. Something about the look in his eyes made me want to tell him everything.

"I ask one thing of you... Please do not tell the Priests of the Shadow coven that I'm here. If you can do that, I will tell you why I left." I bargained.

"I won't tell the Priests of the Shadow coven you're here." He agreed.

"Okay... okay." I took a deep breath, "My mother, Thomia De Valois was the Priestess of the Shadow coven for seven years.

She replaced the previous Priestess when she died in a strange accident. The Priests seemed nice enough, but when another accident happened and my mother died as well…" I swallowed hard. My mother's death had haunted me for years. I could still see her unrecognizable body in my mind's eye. "I was barely twenty-five. The shadows have always favored me. It was expected I'd be the next Priestess. I approached the Priests… I asked them to step down so that Sihr and I could transition into power together. They laughed at me." Anger rose in my chest, and I couldn't keep speaking. The helplessness I'd felt that day enraged me, no one had ever made me feel that way before or again. I would never cower the way I had then.

Something in my eyes must have given away what happened next, "What did they do?" Alok growled. His grip on my wrists tightened, pulling me closer to him.

"They beat me until I couldn't move. The only reason they didn't rape and kill me is because shadows attacked them. My shadows somehow dragged me away. I didn't stop running until I crossed into Georgia. The Priestess of the Blood coven granted me refuge when she saw me." I finished, tears running down my face.

Alok pulled me into his chest, holding me gently even as I felt the tension in his body. "I am sorry. If I had known I would have handled getting you back here differently. I hope with time you'll understand why I've handled your return this way."

"I have to leave, Alok. The Priests are dangerous." I said, panicked. He didn't understand. I couldn't stay here, even if some part of me wanted to.

"They will not touch you." He growled, "There's something I need to tell you, but you have to be willing to listen to me."

"What?" I said, pulling away from him.

"Sihr and I... We are the Priests of Shadow now." He revealed. "And we need you."

Alok

My cheek still stung from the slap Larissa had delivered when I admitted to being the Priest of Shadow. I couldn't blame her anger at my deception. Though some part of me had wanted to turn her over my knee for the slap. I needed to give her time. I was still fuming about her story about the former Priests when Sihr appeared in my bedroom doorway. His dreads were pulled back from his face, and the thin sheen of sweat across his body let me know he'd gone for a run. I wasn't surprised. He was avoiding Larissa. She was nothing like I'd expected. In fact, there was an air of sweetness about her that made me want to protect her from harm.

"How is our captive?" Sihr finally asked, flopping into a chair.

"Don't call her that. She will be our Priestess soon enough. That is deserving of respect." I hoped he'd actually listen. His feelings about Larissa were complicated and he was letting hatred for his father twist the way he viewed her. Yes, she'd disappeared, but I knew she had a good reason. I just didn't feel right telling him what she'd shared with me. "She's not too happy right now, but we had a half decent conversation. I think she will see reason with a little time."

"A little time is all we have, Alok. If she can't see reason, we may have to force her hand." He responded.

I was afraid on exactly how he would do that. Larissa was already traumatized by what had been done to her by Damon and Malik. If Sihr showed her that same type of behavior she would run, and we would never find her. My heart sped up at the idea of losing her already. It was stupid, I barely knew the tiny woman, but some part of me already felt like she was mine. She would be soon enough, I'd ensure that. "We'll talk to her in a bit."

"We don't have too much time for talking." Sihr growled, standing to pace, "Why is she being like this? She was always so logically when we were kids."

She still was, but I couldn't explain that to him without sharing her story. It wasn't my place to do so. Larissa had to be honest with Sihr on her own, I couldn't interfere in their relationship. "Maybe there's more to the story than we know. Give her the benefit of the doubt. We know she's powerful, if she wanted to leave, she already would have. Some part of her still views this at home." I hoped Sihr would listen to me, but the coldness in his eyes as he looked at me didn't bode well.

"We will see." He said, before leaving the room. I glanced down at the shadows trailing behind his feet. I doubted he even realized he'd summoned them, but instead of following him, they departed headed toward Larissa's room.

I grinned. Whether Sihr could admit it yet or not he still cared for her. All I needed to do was stay calm and be reasonable. They would clash first, but it was necessary. They had a history that needed to be resolved before they could move forward. They had me to guide them until then. Together the three of us could save the Shadow coven. I was certain of it.

Four

I was locked in the room again. Apparently, Alok didn't like the slap across the face he'd gotten when he'd finally told me the truth. Whether he lied by omission or not, I didn't care. He'd shown me his true colors when he hadn't immediately told me that he was the new Priest of Shadow. I don't know what they think they need me for, but I'm not going to become their powerful puppet. I needed my freedom. I couldn't end up like my mother, a shriveled husk because two men were hungry for my power. A day passed in silence, and I began to itch to escape the confines of the space. While it might be luxurious, I wasn't meant to be cooped up in a room alone for days on end. My shadows danced from my frustration, twining around my ankles as I paced the floor again.

A quiet knock on the door drug me out of my angry thoughts. They didn't wait for a response, Sihr and Alok appeared before me. In a way, the two men couldn't be more different. Light and dark. Lithe and muscular. A blade and a shield. Yet somehow, they were perfectly in sync as they moved before the bed.

"We need to talk, and you're going to listen." Sihr demanded. He hadn't changed much in the last three years. Standing beside Alok made him seem small, but he was almost six feet tall and built like a runner. His arms were more defined than they had been the last time I'd seen him. His dreads had gotten longer, but the soulful dark eyes that glared at me now were the same one's I'd stared into for hours as a teenager. I couldn't bring myself to speak, seeing him brought back too many memories. Good and bad. When I ran, I hadn't considered how he would take it, but the sneer on his face as he took me in told me everything I needed to know. "You are marked to be the Priestess of this coven. The shirking of your duty has been unacceptable. You will take your place, because if you don't, we will report your lack of coven status to the Hex Guard."

Alok's eyes widened, "Hold on, Sihr. That not how I—"

"Call them. I'd rather them take me away than be stuck in a coven with you." I snapped. I knew the words weren't true, but his behavior hurt. I wasn't going to accept being forced into my role. I'd rather die.

"Wait a second—" Alok looked panicked, but once again he was interrupted.

"You're a fucking brat. I don't know why you ran. I don't care. You shame yourself and your family with your actions. I can have the De Valois thrown from this coven and shunned if I want to."

I felt the blood drain from my face, "You wouldn't dare. After everything my family has done for you." I growled.

"Test me, little witch. See if I have an ounce of empathy for you." Sihr growled, towering over me. "You have one week until we make the announcement. You can stay locked in here if you want, but those are your only options."

"Doesn't sound like a choice at all. Go ahead and make that phone call. They can throw me in a prison cell." I crossed my arms, refusing to budge. If Sihr wanted unreasonable I would show him just how unreasonable I could be.

Alok sighed, "This is not the way." He grabbed Sihr's shoulder, pulling him away from me, "Will you please let me talk to Larissa alone? I'm sure that we can come to a reasonable conclusion to this conversation." Sihr grunted but stormed out of the room without argument. Alok sat heavily on the end of the bed, running his long fingers through his hair. "I don't know y'all's history, but I have a feeling it's going to make this process much harder." He didn't speak for a long time, so I went back to pacing around the room. Alok sighed again before he finally spoke, "I'm an orphan, I don't even know what happened to my parents. I grew up in Florida. You know there isn't much of a magic community down there. When my magic manifested, the Priest of the Siren Coven insisted that I leave the state. Apparently, they'd never had a shadow warlock manifest in that area. Didn't know how to deal with it. I roamed around states until I came across Priest Malik." I shivered at the mention of the Priest's name, "I knew he wasn't a nice man the moment I spoke to him, but he offered me acceptance. He told me that they needed someone of my abilities to fill a power vacuum that had been left behind." He finally met my eyes, "I didn't know until a few months ago that the power vacuum was you. I understand why you left. I believe what you told me."

"Gee thanks." I said, drily. Though my heart fluttered just a little at those words. I didn't know that being believed was one of my hang ups until Alok shined a light on my darkness.

"You have no reason to trust me. You've been hurt by men in my position before, but if you would just consider trying, I can prove to you that I'm nothing like them. I know Priest Damon was Sihr's father, but I don't see the same darkness in Sihr." He continued, twisting his body to stare at me. He was right of course. Sihr was nothing like Damon. "If you can find it in your heart to give us a chance, we can bring the Shadow Coven back to its full power. We can do better than those that came before us."

My chest squeezed at his words. The offer he made seemed genuine. I could see the stress in the tightness of his face. Some quiet part of me wanted to reach out and ease those lines. One of my shadows curled around his wrist, before floating up and caressing his cheek. "You seem like a good man, Alok."

He chuckled, "I am chaotic darkness, Larissa. Don't think for a moment that my desire to have you is out of the kindness of my heart."

"We are part of the darkness. That doesn't make us evil. Without us the light can't shine." I countered. A tense silence filled the room, sexual energy swirling around us. I wanted this man whether I liked it or not, and I was stuck here. Probably forever. I might as well learn to love it. If the choice was to stay a prisoner or become a powerful Priestess... there was no choice at all.

"Why not tell Sihr the truth of why you left?" He asked, changing the subject suddenly.

I shifted, "Sihr loved his father, even if he was a horrid man. If he knew what happened that night, he couldn't live with himself."

"Damon and Malik are still alive." Alok revealed, standing. "It's one of the reasons we need you. Sihr and I can't stabilize the coven without your help. We aren't as powerful as they were. The only reason I was able to run them out was sheer rage."

My eyebrows shot up. I had assumed that the former Priests had died or stepped down willingly, "What happened?" What could Alok have done that had run the Priests off? I didn't have the same gift of Other sight that most witches had, I could occasionally use it, but it was rare and exhausting. Was Alok so full of power that Damon and Malik had run in fear? The man sitting before me didn't exude that kind of energy. Sure, he was clearly strong, but I was certain I would take him in a fair fight easily.

"I found them hurting one of the younger female coven members. She wasn't even old enough to ascend." His jaw muscle jumped, anger lining his entire face, "I don't even know exactly what I did. Sihr only saw the tail end, but enough that he agreed that I had done the right thing."

"I'm sorry." I said, walking over to rest a hand on his shoulder, "You're both too young to be responsible for an entire coven." Priests usually had years of training under the previous leader before they took over a coven.

"That's why we need you." Alok said. He pulled me into him, resting his head against my chest. I almost pushed him away, but this was the first time I'd been touched by a man in longer than I wanted to admit, "Give me a chance. I can give you the life you want, all you have to do is tell me what it is that you desire."

"And if I desire you... and him?" I couldn't believe the words leaving my mouth, but I didn't stop, "It's not common."

"*Anything* you desire." He said, "I need you." The words held far more meaning than I was willing to consider. I didn't give myself more time to think as I grabbed his face in my hands, pressing my lips to his. Before I could prepare for what was coming, he stood, lifting me up. I wrapped my legs around his waist, feeling the growing erection press into my covered pussy. "I wanted you the moment your shadows wrapped around my neck."

"Then have me." I moaned. It was all he needed to launch into action. Breath left me as he threw me onto the bed, shadows wrapped around my arms and legs holding me spread eagle and Alok looked down on me.

"I'm going to undress you. Then my shadows and I will explore every inch of your body slowly and thoroughly until you are begging for my cock." He said, a glint in his eyes. I was surprised by the show of dominance, but it was not unwelcome. I could be in charge in the bedroom, but I did prefer to submit.

His hands were warm as he ran them over my sides, reaching my pants and yanking them down in one move. He tossed them over his shoulder before moving on to my top. Instead of taking it off himself, a shadow appeared between my breasts, shredding through my shirt's material and leaving me bare. The shadow branched out encircling both of my nipples. The feeling was like nothing I'd ever felt, each movement went straight to my core, causing me to squirm. The binds on my hands and feet tightened forcing me to be still as the shadows continued their torture.

"Alok please touch me," I gasped.

He chuckled, darkly, "In time, baby, but I want you begging for me before I've laid a finger on you."

"I am begging," I whined.

"You can do better." He laughed, leaning over to press his lips to my forehead.

I felt a cool touch on my lower belly before it dived down, sliding through my folds and prodding at my entrance. I gasped again, moving my hips to welcome it in. The movement caused it to leave, teasing my thighs and ass instead. I groaned, "Daddy please."

Alok inhaled sharply, "Say it again."

"Daddy, please touch me. I want your cock inside me." I begged.

He groaned, and then he was above me naked. His large cock dripping with pre cum as he pressed gently against my lips. I opened, allowing him to enter my throat. I forced my throat to relax, taking every inch, he offered. My hips bucked wildly as his warms fingers parted my pussy, "Such a swollen and ready little thing. You're taking my cock so well in your throat. Are you ready for me to please you?"

I gurgled around his cock, spit dripping out the sides of my mouth. Finally, he ran his tongue gently over my clit and I saw stars. He forced my hips still with a strong hand as he devoured me. I couldn't breathe, but I didn't care as my orgasm came closer and closer. A cool sensation against my entrance had me pressing down. It pushed in slowly at first and then roughly, filling every inch of me. I'd never felt so full in my life. When another shadow pressed against my back hole I whined, trying to get away. Alok stopped, "Sh, sh, little one. You will take me there as well. Maybe not today, but you'll need to be prepared." Something about his voice made me relax, and I allowed the small shadow to press ever so gently into my ass. Alok began lapping at my clit faster, pushing me to the edge again and again, until finally I erupted. His cock in my throat as the shadows pumped into my other holes was too much. I screamed around him as my orgasm had me lifting my hips off the bed. The movement didn't stop him as he continued to lick until I was shaking and straining to get away.

Carefully he got up, banishing the shadows and leaving me feeling empty. He lifted him into his arms before gathering me onto his lap and laying back, "Ride me." He commanded.

I was still shaking, but I couldn't disobey him, so I sat up, lining my pussy up and slowly sinking down on his cock. Even with my orgasm and the shadow preparation he was large. I hissed as I stretched around him. "What a good girl you can be. Taking every inch of me like that." He gripped my ass forcing me to ride him harder. "But I love it when you're naughty. It gives me a reason to punish you." I moaned at his words, "Oh, you like that don't you? You want me to punish you when you're naughty? I would love to put you over my knee and turn that beautiful ass red with my hand."

I pumped my hips faster, taking him even deeper. His words were lightning to my pussy, and I felt the beginning of another orgasm building. "Please fill me with your cum, daddy. I need it."

He groaned, holding me still as he slammed up into me. My breasts jumped with each thrust, and I threw my head back when a shadow appeared between us, circling my clit. "Cum on my cock, Mommy. Daddy will fill your little hole full."

His words were all I needed to send me over the edge again. My spine bowed as my orgasm rushed over me. Within moments Alok's shouts of pleasure joined my own. Purple light burst around us, and my heart gave a strange tug. I collapsed onto his chest unable to support my body any longer.

"What was that?" Alok panted.

I couldn't respond at first, unsure myself until I felt another strange tug in my chest. My eyes widened, "You're my witch bond."

"Your what?" He asked, his eyebrows furrowing together.

"Witch bonds. It's believed that the Mother and Father share the first bond. They bless witches and warlocks with their own version of the bond when two compatible witches perform a ritual together." I explained.

"I know that. We didn't perform any magic, it's not possible." He pointed out.

"I know... but this feeling is exactly how it was explained to me." I rolled off of him, laying on my back as my mind whirled. I couldn't leave now even if I wanted to. Alok would be able to find me using the bond.

"This is wonderful," Alok said suddenly, turning to look at me, "I couldn't be more thrilled to be bonded to you."

I gave him a small smile, "If this is what the Mother and Father want for us than so it shall be."

He pulled me into his arms, tugging me against his large body. We laid like that for a long time, before I finally dozed off.

Five

The pulsing in my chest the next morning had me on edge. I knew what it meant, but I didn't know what to make of it. Witch bonds required magic to complete, Alok and I hadn't performed a spell together. The sex had been transcendent, but sex revealing a witch bond was unheard of. I stared down at his sleeping face, unsure if I should wake him or not.

"Staring at someone while they sleep is serial killer behavior." He said, groggily.

"You kidnapped me." I pointed out. I knew I should have felt more upset by what Alok and Sihr had done, but I knew they were desperate. It didn't completely excuse them, but I should never have run away in the first place. The Shadow Coven was mine and I'd let it suffer under the hands of monsters for long enough.

He shrugged his shoulder as he turned on his side to look at me. After a moment his eyes widened, "Do you feel it to?" I swallowed, giving him a nod. "You're mine." He growled, running a hand over my collarbone, "Forever." He stopped to think for a moment, "The bond will form with Sihr as well."

My eyes widened, "That's not possible."

"Of course it is. Haven't you ever read about the Amor Coven in France? It's run by a witch and four warlocks that are all bonded." Alok explained.

"You can't know that Sihr…" I trailed off. I'd loved Sihr since I was sixteen. We'd never slept together. Though we'd certainly come close a few times, but our parents had been insistent that we both wait. Long past the point that we were old enough to enjoy each other we had waited. It felt romantic then, that one day our first time would be in honor of our ascension to priesthood. Now it felt like a waste.

"You already know." He grinned. "This is perfect. He'll be so happy, it's fantastic news."

"Wait, Alok. We can't tell him yet. You need to give him and I time to work out our… issues." I insisted.

"You have until the eclipse. I can put off his timeline that long, but we need to the coven to be back at full power by then." Alok offered. My nerves skyrocketed. Eclipses were sacred to shadow witches, our magic seemed to rise to the surface. I had no idea there was one coming up so soon.

"Why?" I asked.

"Because it's been a year since we removed Malik and Damon from power. There's been rumblings that they are going to come for us. I think it'll be on the anniversary." He explained. "The veil between us and our magic will be thinner. It's the perfect time for them to strike."

"Fuck." I breathed out. He was right, the veil between our world and the realm of the Mother and Father would be thin. Our magic was more powerful when we could draw more closely from the source. If Malik and Damon were overpowered when they came at us, I didn't know that we would be able to stop them.

"That's exactly what we're about to do." He grinned, distracting me from his very short timeline.

The next three days passed in relative peace. I chose to stay in my room mostly, ignoring the fact that I needed to rejoin my coven. I didn't know if I could face my former friends that I had left behind. If Sihr carried such negative opinions of me, I'm sure most of the coven did as well. I couldn't imagine telling them why I left, it had been hard enough sharing with Alok. Just the thought of his name caused my chest to squeeze. He was my witch bond, but we hadn't performed a spell together. It made no sense, yet I couldn't deny the way I felt.

My door swung open, and I was suddenly bombarded by a yelling child. "Ris, Ris. You're finally home!" I recognized the adorable lisp of my niece, Annette.

"Oh my, you've gotten so big." I exclaimed, picking her up. "How old are you now?"

"I'm seven. You should know that, you sent me a birthday card just last month." She pointed out.

"I guess I did. How did you get here?" I glanced out the open door but found the hallway empty.

"Daddy told me to come get you." She explained.

"Laurence is here?" I asked but immediately started down the stairs. This was the first time I'd been outside my room since coming here. My meals always appeared outside the door, or Alok brought them himself. I'd realized a few days before that I was in the coven home that Malik and Damon had purchased. Clearly Sihr and Alok had made some upgrades. The wallpaper was a soft grey color; plush black carpet lined the stairs. The place looked like the mansion of shadow witches without a doubt.

"Now there's my adorable little sister," Laurence's voice boomed, "I was wondering when Alok and Sihr would finally let you out."

I grinned, sitting down my niece to embrace my big brother. It was the first time I'd seen him in almost four years. I took him in. He shared the same skin tone and eye shape, but that was where our similarities needed. He looked like a carbon copy of our Papa. "You shaved your head."

"Babette made me." He griped, his dark brown eyes filling with fondness for his wife. "You look even smaller. Have you lost weight? They are feeding you, right?"

"They are feeding me, but what were you planning to do if they weren't? We both know you'd never lay a hand on Sihr." I joked.

"If he hurts my baby sister, I'll feed him to my gators." He responded seriously. He dropped his voice, "I know you aren't back willingly. Do you need help?"

I chewed my lip, "I'm okay, Laury."

"Ugh I hate that nickname." He groaned.

"Laury, Laury, Laury." Annette sung as she skipped around us.

Laurence groaned again but changed the subject. "Dad and Gramma will be here soon. Alok invited us to have dinner with you."

"Oh." Dread filled my stomach. I wasn't ready to face all of my family. I had kept them at a distance, treating them horribly for years now. Would they ever be able to forgive me?

"Hey, it's okay. We have just missed you." Laurence wrapped an arm around my shoulders. "I need to know what you've been up to the last few years."

I forced myself to relax, as I told Laurence bits of pieces of my life since I ran away. I ensured to only tell him the good parts. We had taken seats in a small den connected to the dining room. The front door closing stopped our conversation, causing me to straighten my spice. I waited with bated breath as my father and grandmother made their way to us. The moment I saw their faces my eyes filled with tears.

"Oh, my little boo. Come here." Gramma opened her thin arms, pulling me in immediately. Tears ran down my face as her bergamot scent filled my nose. "I've missed you so much, Cher. You broke my old heart."

Eventually I pulled away from her, wiping the tears from my face. Before I could recover my father pulled me into his arms, "My little Ris, you look more and more like your mama everyday."

"It's good to see you, Papa," I dropped my voice, "Why didn't you tell me about Alok and Sihr?"

"I was told not to." He responded, looking away. I furrowed my eyebrows, but didn't have a chance to respond before Sihr and Alok entered the room we'd taken over.

Gramma was the first to speak, "Priests, we didn't expect you to be joining us today."

Alok opened his mouth to speak, but Sihr responded first, "Larissa cannot be trusted, so we're here to make sure she doesn't convince anyone to help her escape."

My mouth dropped open at his words, as rage consumed me, "Really? How dare you speak to her that way." Shadows rushed around me as my magic responded to my emotions. Sihr tried to speak, but shadows rushed into his opened mouth muffling his words, "If I am to be Priestess of the Shadow Coven, you will treat me and my family with respect." I didn't consider that I'd never confirmed that I would take on my role. With that single sentence I had sealed my fate.

Sihr's own shadows lashed out, pushing mine away. I braced myself for an attack, but none ever came. He simply turned on his heel and stomped out of the room.

"Well now that that unpleasantness is out of the way. It's nice to finally meet each of you. Obviously, you know that I am Priest Alok. Welcome to our home, dinner will be served shortly. Please follow me to the dining room." Alok said, motioning for us to follow him, "I hope everyone enjoys catfish."

"Son, it's okay to touch my daughter. Witch bonds are hard to ignore." Papa said, causing me to gasp.

"How can you tell?" I hissed, "We haven't even sealed the bond yet."

"Then the Mother and Father have blessed you!" Papa said, excitedly.

"Paul, calm down. Can't you see that you're freaking the girl out." Gramma interrupted, "Take your time with the bond, Larissa."

"I am blessed by the Mother and Father, because they brought Rissa into my life. I hope we have your blessing as well." Alok said, looking between my father and grandmother.

"As long as my girl is happy, I'll be glad for her." Gramma said, wrapping an arm around me.

"I'll do everything in my power to keep her happy." Alok responded, seriously.

Thankfully two maids entered the room, placing dishes in front of each of us. I wasn't sure how I felt about Alok's declaration. I didn't love him yet, but I felt a strange stirring in my chest every time his green eyes met mine.

"Aunt Rissa, why did you leave anyway?" Annette asked, breaking the silence.

"Annette, that's rude to ask." Laurence chastised

"She's just a child, Laurence. They ask the questions us adults are thinking." Gramma said, looking at me.

I stuffed a fork full of fish into my mouth to avoid answering the question. Alok looked at me with sad eyes, but I could tell he wanted me to tell my family why I'd actually left.

"I ran after an... incident with Damon and Malik." I said, vaguely.

Papa growled, "What did they do? Why didn't you come to me?"

I glanced to my niece, "It's best if we don't get into details now...."I trailed off considering his question. It had never crossed my mind to tell my family the truth of why I had left. Giving them impossible conditions for my return had been far easier, "I didn't want to risk your lives."

Everyone stared at me in silence for several long moments, before Laurence finally spoke, "I would have done anything to protect you, Ris. I hope you'll consider that in the future. We'd rather have you here and fight for you than worry about your well being."

"No one will need to fight for her well being." Alok assured everyone.

"You may be a Priest, but even you cannot guarantee her safety." Gramma said, "You should have been training your powers these last three years."

"I have been." I defended.

"Have you tested her?" Gramma asked, ignoring me.

"I've had no need. She has made her control of her powers very clear. Obviously when she becomes Priestess there will be growth, but I'm certain she can handle it." Alok replied.

Gramma hummed, clearly mulling over his words, "We shall see. When is the ceremony planned for?"

"Five more days." Alok said. My heart rate sped up, I hadn't realized we were so close.

"She'll need to see the coven before she takes the role on." Papa said, "I can plan that if it would help."

"Please, I am still getting to know everyone and Sihr... Well we have some things to work out between now and then." He said.

I snorted. I couldn't imagine how we were going to work out all of our issues between now and then, but it seemed like Alok had a plan. I needed to talk to Sihr, but every time I saw him there were too many feelings to deal with. He had every right to be angry with me. I had abandoned him, had broken my promises. When we were children, Sihr never wanted to become Priest even though it was always clear he would follow in his father's footsteps. Somehow I would have to get him to understand my side of the story, to see why I left.

Conversation swirled around me, and slowly I relaxed. Being with my family and Alok was a breath of fresh air. I loved my time with the Blood Coven, but I had always been an outsider. Only Bambi was unperturbed by my presence. I missed my friend, I wondered if she'd gone to my apartment yet. Hopefully she would understand why I left. At some point I'd reach out and let her know I was okay, but I had to handle everything here first.

Hours passed as Gramma and Papa told stories of my childhood. Laurence carried Annette, her soft snores were adorable. "It was good to see you. Have us over again soon. Preferably after you've dealt with your... man drama."

"Next time bring Babette." I insisted, ignoring his words.

He pressed a kiss to my cheek before leaving. Gramma and Papa both wrapped me in tight hugs, promises of more visits escorted them out the door.

I sighed loudly as Alok locked the door, "I love them, but I remember why I enjoyed being away now."

"You'll never be far from them now." Alok growled, scooping me into his arms, "I'd like to ravish you now, but I've got some work to do. I am going to tuck you into bed."

"I can get myself to bed." I argued, wiggling in his arms.

"Of course you can, but I want to treat you like the princess that you are." He said.

"What happened to calling me mommy?" I asked, remembering the night on my balcony.

His cheeks turned pink, "Well when a badass woman starts choking you out... Things are said."

"Maybe I liked it." I said, running my nails down the back of his neck.

"You keep doing that and I'm not going to be able to leave you alone." He growled.

I grinned as he sat me down on the bed, "But you have work to do. I guess I'll just have to take care of myself tonight."

His pupils dilated, a rumble starting in his chest as he loomed over me. "You won't touch yourself unless I'm there to watch."

I smirked, "How will you know if I do?"

"I have my ways." He said mysteriously. "If you're a good girl I'll reward you, but if not I'll have to punish you."

"Maybe I should punish you for making me wait." I shot back.

He just smirked at me before exiting the room. I debated for a long moment if I wanted to push the limits. Ultimately, I decided to see what reward he'd give me later.

Six

Two more days passed with relative quiet. I now had full access to the house, so I explored every nook and cranny. I hardly ever saw anyone other than Alok, but I didn't mind the quiet. My anxiety was high, my shadows more and more restless as we approached the day of my joining the coven.

"What are you doing in here?" Sihr's voice caused icy chills to run down my spine.

"I live here." I responded, ignoring him. I continued to run my paintbrush over the canvas I'd uncovered while I explored the basement.

"That doesn't look like anything." He sneered.

I paused, setting my paintbrush down. I took a deep breath before turning to face him, "Trying to tear me apart isn't going to make you feel any better."

He crossed his arms, "Maybe not, but maybe you deserve to feel half of what I felt when I found out you ran off without saying a word."

"I'm sorry." I said, refusing to look away from the dark depths of his eyes, "I didn't do it to hurt you. I should have found a way to reach you. I broke my promises to you, and I understand why you're angry with me."

"You understand nothing, Larissa." He growled. "If you knew what I went through after you left…"

"Tell me," I ground out, frustration bubbling up, "But have you ever considered why I left?"

"The reason doesn't matter." He snapped, "Go back to your fucking painting."

He went to storm out of the room, but I was hot on his heels, "Look who is running now."

He spun on me, but before he could respond the house shook causing me to tumble forward into his chest. He caught me, pulling me in close as pictures crashed to the ground around us. Shadows coalesced around us, protecting us from the falling debris. The warmth of his body was familiar and yet somehow it felt completely foreign. I looked up into his eyes, finding him staring back at me. An unspoken conversation passed between us, years of pain we'd carried. I opened my mouth to say something... anything, but I was cut off.

"Rissa, Sihr," I heard Alok shout, so I forced my way out of Sihr's arms. I waved the shadows away, rushing toward his voice. "They're here." Alok was pale and panting when we found him in the main foyer.

Sihr cursed, "We aren't ready to deal with this."

"They know that. Someone must have told them that we're going to have our Priestess soon." Alok said.

I ground my teeth together, putting the pieces together. Malik and Damon were causing this, they had come for us. "I'm going outside."

"Oh, hell no you aren't." Alok grabbed for me, but I was faster. I ducked under his arms and was gone before he could chase me.

I threw open the front doors, stepping outside. The lawn was covered in angry shadows, but I ignored them as I stormed to the two older men standing in the center of our front lawn. "Larissa

De Valois, I'd heard rumors you'd returned." Malik sneered at my approach.

"And I've heard rumors you were unseated by an orphaned warlock." I snapped, "Seems like an embarrassment to show your faces here doesn't it?"

He lunged at me, but my shadows lashed out. He howled as he pulled away, dark marks on his exposed ankles. "Don't worry you're pretty little head about that, cher. We'll have you back in our hands soon enough." Damon said. I took him in. Sihr looked so much like his father, but the difference was Damon's eyes were dead. There was no life or emotion behind them. The only time I'd ever seen him show any emotion is the glee on his face as he loomed over my beaten body, "You weren't strong enough to beat us before. Neither was the orphan or my pathetic son. With this eclipse we will take back the Shadow Coven. And with you as our Priestess we will be the most powerful coven in the Northern Hemisphere."

I forced myself to remain calm, "I'll see you in two days then. We'll be ready to find out just how powerful you two are." They would never see my fear again. I would erase them from existence, or I would return to the Mother and Father in two days. I turned on my heel, giving them my back as I walked toward Sihr and Alok. Both of the men were stony faced, but I could see the shock in their eyes at my words.

"Oh don't worry, we'll be seeing you very soon." Malik said, before they both dissolved into shadow.

"I really need to learn that trick." I muttered as I walked back into the house. I could use my shadows as weapons or to gather intel without a second thought, but I had never mastered shadow walking.

"What the fuck were you thinking?" Sihr shouts from behind me, as his warm hand wraps around my bicep spinning me around,

"They will eat you alive, Ris. We aren't prepared to fight them, certainly not before you've taken your place within the coven."

"Then I guess we'll just have to hasten my ascension won't we." I snap, "Or would that fuck up all the anger and hate that you have toward me?"

"I don't hate you." He said, staring down at me, "Tell me why you left."

"No." I pull away from him, taking the stairs two at a time. I could hear him storming after me, but I ignored it. Before I could slam my bedroom door in his face, he slid past me, forcing himself in my path. I stop, crossing my arms over my chest, "Get out of my room."

"No." He said, "I deserve answers, Larissa."

"You haven't wanted answers until now, Sihr. In fact, even when I didn't run, you've continued to treat me like I'm a monster... Maybe I am." I deflate at my words. Some part of me knew that I was a monster for leaving him behind with his father. I could have come back at any time.

"Do you know how hard it was for me when you left? The ridicule I've received from our peers. They all assumed you left because you didn't want to be my Priestess." Sihr admitted.

"What? How does that even make sense? Your father was still Priest when I left." I argue.

"Facts don't matter. You should know that better than anyone." He growled.

I sighed, "The night I left... Sihr... Damon and Malik are the reason my mother is dead." The room filled with silence, neither of us even dared to breathe as I continued, "I would never have been your Priestess. They would have drained me just like they had your mother, Priestess Hera, and my mother."

I saw rage in his eyes as he stared at me. I prepared myself for the blow. Instead a single tear rolled down his face, "What happened that night, my ombra."

Hearing the nickname he'd called me since we were children softened my heart, "I asked them to step down so that you and I could take over the Shadow coven together."

His eyebrows rose, "You didn't discuss that with me."

"It's common for priests to step down if the next priestess is significantly younger than them. They generally help pave the way for the Priestess' witch bond." I explained, "I had read that a few weeks before my mother died. She always had me doing research on covens."

A small smile showed on his face, "Thomia was always good to me." A look of guilt flashed in his eyes, "You presented them this evidence?"

I nodded, "They weren't ever going to give up their power, Sihr. The only reason I got away is the shadow's protection."

We were silent for a long moment, "My father put his hands on you." He finally growled, "Did he..." He trailed off unable to ask.

"They were going to. I got away before they had the chance." I said, laying a hand over his, "I am sorry for leaving Sihr. I... I understand if you can't forgive me."

He pulled away, pacing the room for several tense minutes. "I've hated for you three years." My heart stopped in my chest at his words. I knew they were true. I'd seen the hate in his eyes more than once since they'd brought me back here. I couldn't truly blame him. I gasped as he swept me into his arms, "I allowed my love for you to be twisted, my ombra. Allowed the words of others to cloud my mind. I need to earn your forgiveness."

I smoothed my hand over his locs, playing with some of the golden jewels attached for a long moment, "I am not angry with you, Sihr. I only wish for us to move forward. The coven needs us."

"Fuck the coven." He growled. His lips crashed into mine, the taste of him bringing back a hundreds memories. I wrap my arms around his neck, letting him take on all of my weight. "I have wanted you for so long. I'm done asking."

I moaned as he bit down on my neck. I could tell it's going to leave a bruise, but I don't care. I need to feel him in every possible way. I need to inhale his very essence. He tosses me down on the bed, and I'm on my knees crawling toward him in moments. I grip his shirt, yanking it over his head. He rips away my clothes like a mad man, leaving him in a pile on the floor. He stops me when I reach for the button of his jeans, "You always come first." With that, he's pushing me backwards, spreading my legs apart. "Such a pretty little pussy. It's haunted my dreams for three years that I've never had a taste of you." His tongue at my entrance causes me to arch off the bed. I don't even know how I'm already this close. Sihr is nothing like Alok in bed, but somehow it's exactly what I wanted. He slows down, lapping me slowly, twirling his tongue over my clit. My eyes pop open as I realize, "Sihr, stop I need to tell you something."

He sits up, "What is wrong, ombra?"

"Alok and I share a witch bond." I blurt out.

The emotion on his face gutters out, "I see." His hand resting on my thigh grips tighter, "I won't search for my witch bond if that is your concern. You are my Priestess. That is all that matters to me. Sex will strength the coven's bond."

My chest constricts, "I don't care about that, Sihr. I want you for you... I... I have loved you since we were children. A witch bond could never change that."

"Lay back, let me bring you pleasure." Sihr said, dismissing our conversation.

I don't feel good about it, but the feelings he invokes as he returns to his task are overwhelming. My legs shake as I get closer and closer to the edge, "Please, Sihr. Please."

"Beg me for your orgasm, ombra." He growls into my pussy.

"Please, let me cum. I need to cum." I screamed when my release finally rushes down my spine. Lights dancing behind my eyes as I arch up, my orgasm forcing me to move.

I'm spent and panting, unable to even think when Sihr flips me onto my belly. He grips my hips, forcing me onto my knees. "I am going to take you now. You will belong to me in every way that matters. You will spend the rest of your life with my cum dripping from your perfect little pussy." With those words he slams into me. My vision whites out as his huge cock bumps into my cervix. The pain and pleasure combined have me wailing, incomprehensible begging leaving my mouth. A series of slaps on my ass bring me back to my body as he continues to drive into me. "I own you, Larissa De Valois. Never again will you be away from my side." When I only moan in response, his hand slaps down on my ass again, "Say it."

"You own me." I grunt.

"Again." He punctuates his demand with another series of slaps. My ass is throbbing as his cock pounds into me.

Tears drips down my face, "Sihr you own me. I am yours from now until the Father takes me."

"I will bring you back if He doesn't take me too." He growls, pulling me up by my hair, "You will wear my marks, you will drip with my cum. You. Are. Mine." With his words he pounds into me deeper until finally I feel his hot seed spill into me.

We crashed down onto the bed, his body partially covering mine as we both pant. "That was better than I imagined." Sihr said, pressing a kiss to my temple.

"Better than your hand I'm sure." I joked, sitting up, "We need to clean up and go talk to Alok."

He groaned, "Can't you give me a few more minutes to recover?"

Seeing him relaxed was nice. I hadn't seen him like his old self since I'd gotten back home. I leaned toward him, pressing my lips to his gently, "I'm glad to be home."

Seven

"**E**veryone quiet!" Alok shouted over the entire coven. The voices had been pounding at my head for the last fifteen minutes, but I couldn't bring myself to complain. "We wanted to gather all of you and speak about the coven."

"We aren't a coven without a Priestess." Someone shouts back.

I sighed and stepped forward, "Silence. You're here today to witness Alok, Sihr, and I solidifying my place as Priestess."

The moon hangs high in the sky, giving us more light than usual. The black candles around us flicker ominously as everyone stares at me, "You know who I am. You know that I left three years ago. You've made up many theories on why I might have done that, but I'm here to tell you the truth tonight."

Alok gripped my elbow, and whispered, "They don't deserve your story."

I shake him away, and continued, "I left because Malik and Damon nearly killed me. Just like they killed my mother and their other Priestesses before her."

Gasps and shouts go up among the coven. Most calling for punishment of the old priests, but there is plenty of disbelief woven through, "I cannot provide you proof of this. But look in your hearts, you know that I was chosen to be Priestess by the Mother and Father. Tonight I will show you that."

I turn away from the crowd, calling my shadows forth and reaching for Alok and Sihr. Their large hands give me strength as I begin the ritual, "Mother, I call to you. Father, I call to you." I let my shadows spread out, mingling with Alok's and Sihr's as we circle each other, "We are your loyal servants. We ask that you bless our roles within the Shadow coven so that we may do work in your name." Shadows twist around us, faster and faster causing me to get dizzy. Purple light suddenly bursts in our entwined hands, before shooting straight into our chests. I gasp, but force myself to continue, "I am your Priestess."

"I am your Priest." Alok echoes.

"I am your Priest." Sihr sounds far away as he speaks.

Our voices lift toward the sky, "May we bring honor to your names."

Shadows and purple light shoot up into the sky twisting around. It looks like a tornado in the center of our circle. My heart beats out of my chest, and I squeeze their hands tighter as the tornado suddenly dissipates, rushing back into each of us.

There's a long moment of silence as we stand together still holding hands. I look into their eyes and I know beyond a shadow of a doubt that the Mother and Father have blessed me with two witch bonds. Two men that are forever tied to me, and now we are forever tied to the Shadow coven. Claps break the silence, forcing us to break apart and take in our coven again. As we descend from the dais we had been standing on people bow, a few kissing our hands as we pass.

Gramma and Papa stand at the back, grins splitting both of their faces, "I always knew you'd be something special, boo." Gramma said, pulling me into a hug.

I hug her back, before throwing myself into my father's arms. Tonight was just the beginning of our problems. At least we had the coven's acceptance now, but Damon and Malik would come at us even harder now. I could feel my power under my skin, but I didn't know if it would be enough, "Stop worrying, Larissa. The Mother and Father have blessed us tonight. That is all that matters." Papa whispered.

"Let's enjoy the festivities." I said, pulling away from him.

"I'm exhausted." I said as I throw myself onto my bed. "Are we sure about this whole Priestess thing?"

A sharp slap to my ass caused me to yelp, "You can't get out of this now." Sihr said, sitting down next to me, "You're stuck with both of us."

"Yes, my shadow daddies." I said, heat rushing toward my core as I watched Alok strip out of his shirt.

"Our shadow mommy." Alok said, making his way toward us. "Why is she still dressed?"

Sihr grinned, "That's a good question." Shadows crept toward me, before once again all the clothes I'm wearing are shredded away.

"I've got to learn that trick," I muttered. I wanted to shred the clothes off of these men with my shadows.

"You need to train." Alok said, as he pushed his pants down his hard cock springing up against his stomach.

"I can take your cock just fine." I joked.

"Well, good. I'll be taking your ass tonight," He grinned, before pouncing on me, "Sihr, how shall we service our Priestess first?"

My pussy was wet at the thought of both of them taking me at once, but I couldn't squirm with the way that Alok was holding me in the air legs spread over his arms. "I think I'll have a taste to start." Sihr said, crawling between my legs.

Alok holds me open as Sihr takes his time devouring my pussy. "I'm gonna cum." I moaned.

Sihr pulls away completely causing me to convulse, "She doesn't cum first tonight. Put her on my cock and prep her ass." He demanded as he stretched out, his cock ready for me. Alok guides me down until I'm impaled on his cock and Sihr takes over. The feeling of his cock in my needy pussy has me bouncing quickly. I run hands over his stomach, digging my nails in until I see lines of blood blooming, "I don't like to be denied."

A hand between my shoulder blades pushed me forward. Lubed fingers prod my hole, causing me to squirm, "Relax. I'll make sure you're ready before you take me." I do as he said, forcing my body to relax and focus on the pleasure of both of these men, my men, loving me. He works two fingers in slowly, until I'm moaning and pressing back on them.

"Give me your cock." I growled.

"You're not ready yet," Alok said.

"Just do it. I can take a little pain. I need you inside me." I demanded.

He chuckles, but continues his slow pace. Finally he pulled away, and I take a deep breath when I feel his large cock press against my hole. "You want to take us both."

"Yes please." I moaned.

"Such an eager hole," Alok groans as he pressed further in. Pain zips up my spine at the stretch, but Sihr sucks one of my nipples into his mouth distracting me.

"You can only cum once we're both inside you, ombra." Sihr said, reaching between our bodies and brushing my clit. I force myself to relax, taking every inch of Alok's cock in my ass. The feeling of them both stretching my holes is unholy, but I loved it. Alok begin to fuck me harder, forcing me onto Sihr's cock harder and faster.

"I'm not going to last long," Alok groans.

"I'm with you, bro." Sihr growled back.

They begin fucking me faster, "Play with yourself. I want to see you fall apart with both of us inside you." He commanded.

A few circles of my clit and I'm coming undone, a scream ripping from my throat. "Fuck." Alok and Sihr mutter in unison, as they follow me over the edge.

"Oh fuck." A voice I haven't heard in weeks shouts. I turned my head, Sihr and Alok still inside me to find Bambi and Fang in the door of my bedroom, "I... We heard you scream. I... Just gonna step out in the hall while you... Yup. Come on." Bambi stuttered, before dragging Fang from the room.

"Who the fuck is that?" Sihr growled, lifting me gently away from their cocks.

"That's my best friend." I responded.

"Your best friend is a blood witch and Priestess?" Alok asked as he walked into the bathroom.

Eight

Bambi and Fang were whispering to themselves, glancing around the foyer. Our home was lavish, even more so than the large, plantation style home that Bambi grew up in. I was used to it, since I'd partially grown up within its walls. It was far nicer than the Blood coven's mansion, but not nearly as homey. With time I would change that.

"Rissa, are you okay?" Bambi asked as she launched herself at me, "You can't just disappear without a word and think I'm not going to hunt you down."

"I'm fine, Bams. I'd like to introduce you to, Alok and Sihr," I gestured for them to come forward, "They're my witch bonds."

Bambi gasped, "Both of them?" She glanced toward Fang, and then whispered, "You think everyone has more than one?"

"Don't even think about it, Bambi Cruor. I'd never share you," Fang growled.

She straightened, sending him a glare, "It's nice to meet you both. I'm Bambi Cruor, future Priestess of the Blood coven and this is my witch bond, Fang Boucher."

Alok stepped forward, pulling her into a big hug, "Thank you for being kind to my Rissa."

Fang tensed, but relaxed when Bambi pulled away, "She's my best friend." A look crossed her face, "Why not tell me you were coming back to your coven?"

My face went hot, "Well I…"

"We kidnapped her." Alok said, casually.

"You what?!" Bambi was crossing the small space that separated them. She grabbed him by the shirt, "If she gives me given the smallest hint that she doesn't want to be here, I will drain every drop of blood from your body and bathe in it."

Alok's eyes widened, "Larissa, please call her off."

I laughed, "It's okay, Bambi. We've gotten past the kidnapping."

She stepped away, looking at Fang, "I understand. Fang stalked me."

"I wasn't stalking you. I was just trying to have a conversation, and you made that very difficult." He argued.

"You definitely stalked her. I was there." I pointed out. He winked at me; his sense of humor having grown since being with Bambi. They complimented each other perfectly. It made me wonder how the Mother and Father selected bonds. Clearly, chemistry mattered.

"We can give y'all a guestroom tonight, but you should leave at first light." Sihr interrupted.

"I'd like to stay for a day or two." Bambi said, narrowing her eyes at Sihr, "Make sure Larissa is okay."

"He's right, Bambi. Y'all need to get out of here. We have a situation with the former Priests. I don't want either of you getting caught in the crossfire." I agreed.

"If you're in danger, we aren't going anywhere." She said, waving me off, "A couple of old Priests don't stand a chance against the two of us."

"The five of us," Fang said, nodding to Alok and Sihr, "I agree with her. We can stay and help y'all."

I looked to my men, unsure what to do. I didn't want my friend to get hurt for me, but she was a very powerful witch. "Sleep on it. We can figure everything out in the morning."

Bambi pulled me into another hug, and whispered, "Those two are fine as fuck, Ris. Looked like y'all are getting along just fine."

"I think I might love them." I whispered back.

Bambi pulled away, giving me a look before following a maid to their room for the night. I knew she would have questions for me soon.

I sighed as they disappeared up the stairs, "I'm exhausted. Can we go get some sleep?"

"I'm going to stay up tonight and keep an eye out. Damon and Malik will have heard the news of your ascension." Alok said, pressing a kiss to my forehead.

I woke up alone and strangely cold. I sat up, but when I went to place my feet on the ground, frost covered the floor.

"Sihr? Alok?" I called out, unwilling to set my bare feet on the floor.

Silence was my only answer. I tried to summon my shadows, but I got no response. Panic filled my body, with my hands shaking I wrapped the blanket around my body. I extended my leg as far as possible, using my toes to grab the edge of my shoes. After several minutes of maneuvering, I was able to get both shoes on. With some protection on my feet, I stood from the bed. I crept toward the door, shivering as I opened it.

I screamed when I saw my mother's dead body suspended in the air in front of me. I slammed the door, tears streaking down my face as I ran to the balcony. I threw open the doors, only to find that a void of blackness was all I could see. I backed away, reaching again for my shadows. I felt a sputter of magic building, but something blocked me from it. I grunted in frustration, steeling myself as I headed back to the bedroom door. I forced myself to duck around my mother's desecrated corpse. I walked to the stairs, but stopped when I noticed smoke coming from underneath one of the bedroom doors. I reached for the knob, ignoring the pain as it burned my hand. As the door swung open, I once again screamed. Alok sat in the middle of the room, completely engulfed in flame.

"This is all your fault, Larissa." His voice reaches my ears, "Everyone you care for dies."

I move away, sinking to the ground as tears rush down my face. He was right, everyone near me was in danger. Shadows appear above me, hovering just out of reach. I brought myself to my knees, "Please, please help me."

The shadows swarmed me, but instead of the usual calm and serenity I felt as they melted into my skin, they burned me. I screamed as my skin burned.

"Rissa, Rissa. Wake up, you're having a nightmare," Sihr's voice pulled me out of my sleep. I bolted upright, panting as the images from my dream assaulted me. Sihr pulled me into his lap, holding me as tears continued to run down my face.

"Where is Alok?" I asked, suddenly.

"He's outside working a protection spell." Sihr responded.

I stood, running out the door and down the stairs as fast as my legs could go. My bare feet slapped the concrete of the driveway, as I careened around searching for Alok. Concrete changed to grass and then dirt as I hunted across the property for my witch bond. My shadows slithered along the ground, helping me look for him. I didn't find him anywhere; there was no sign of him on the grounds. I ran back to the house, nearly colliding with Sihr.

The panic in his eyes made my stomach sink, "They took him."

"No. There's no way." I breathed.

"Damon and Malik have Alok. They are demanding that we meet them tonight under the eclipse." Sihr gripped my arms, forcing me to sit down as I continued to panic.

Footsteps down the stairs didn't stop the tears running down my face. "What's going on?" Fang asked.

"The former priests of shadow have taken Alok." Sihr said.

Bambi gasped, rushing to my side, "Don't worry, Ris. We're going to get him back. They've fucked with the wrong witches."

I stared blankly ahead as my emotions numbed out. The two people I feared most in the world had taken my bond. I knew they did it because of me. Everyone I have ever loved suffered because of them. It would end tonight.

Nine

T he sun was hanging low in the sky, as we made our way onto the boat that would take us deeper into the bayou. Sihr and I were visible, while Fang and Bambi had performed a spell to keep themselves hidden from sight. They would only step in if they had to. I had insisted that I would handle them myself. Sihr used magic to guide the boat down the river. I watched as gators swam by. I would become an animal tonight. I would rip Damon and Malik apart with my teeth and bare hands for daring to put a hand on my bond.

"Don't do anything impulsive, ombra. We can take them down together. You are not alone this time," Sihr said. I knew he could read my thoughts easily. It had been nothing for us to fall back into our friendship.

I nodded, unable to promise him anything. When it came to my witch bonds I would do anything for them. I may have only just found them, but I've already wasted three years running away from the people I love. I'm done with that life.

"We're almost there. Can you feel the magic in the air?" Sihr asked.

I unleashed my magic, suffocating underneath the sheer weight of my new power. This is the first time I'd really delved into it since I became Priestess. I could feel what Sihr had mentioned, but I lifted my hand, "Clear out." were the only words I spoke. Shadows shivered in the sky, before completely disappearing, brightening the sky minimally. I glanced up, noting that the moon had appeared. The eclipse would happen soon.

"That was an impressive display of power, Larissa." Damon's voice rang out all around us, "But it won't save your friend."

"Damon, Malik. Show yourselves." I shouted, jumping from the boat before it had reached the rickety dock. "You're cowards for this. You think I don't know that you had a Dream witch attack me?"

I sent shadows searching for them, keeping an eye on the sky. No voices responded, but one of my shadows returned, sinking back into my skin. The image in my brain showed a bloody and bruised Alok, tied to a tree. I didn't hesitate as I beelined in the direction the shadow had taken. I could hear Sihr hot on my heels, but I continued forward, ducking under low hanging branches. We came to a small break in the trees and I saw him. Alok's head was lulled to the side, blood dripping from his temples. His face was swollen and nearly unrecognizable. I rushed toward him, but hit a barrier. I was thrown back, but thankfully Sihr managed to catch me before I flew into a tree.

"We won't make it that easy." Malik appeared a few feet away. Sihr kept a grip on me, making it impossible for me to launch myself at him. "If you want your precious bond back. You will give up your power to us."

"That is an abomination to the Mother and Father," Sihr growled, "She was blessed by them, and you ask her to throw that in their faces?"

Damon appeared next to Malik, and snorted, "The Mother and Father don't give a damn about the witches and warlocks of this world. They are a fairytale to keep you pathetic creatures in line. The Priests carry all the power in this world, and I want it back."

I heard a small rustle in the trees near us, and glanced over, noticing Bambi and Fang's spell had worn off. I forced my eyes forward, hoping Malik and Damon wouldn't notice them. "I'll do it."

"No," Sihr growled, but I slipped away moving toward where Damon and Malik stood, "Larissa don't!"

I called my power to the surface, "What do I have to do?"

"You will perform a ritual with us. During which your power will become ours." Malik responded.

"I'll only do it if you allow Alok and Sihr to leave before we begin." I demanded.

They looked to each other for a moment, "Your friends hidden in the bushes may take Alok away, but Sihr will remain." My heart dropped when he mentioned Bambi and Fang, but I didn't let my emotions show.

I glanced at Sihr. His face was stony, anger radiating from him. "That's acceptable." I waved for Bambi and Fang to come forward. Malik held up his hand, and I watched as the barrier around Alok lifted for Fang and Bambi to enter. I kept my eyes trained on them as they untied Alok and began to carry him out of the clearing. Bambi gave me a sharp nod. She understood better than anyone how powerful a witch bond could be. None of us moved until they had disappeared into the trees surrounding us.

Damon beckoned me forward, but Sihr gripped my bicep, leaning down to whisper, "You don't have to do this."

I stared into his dark eyes for a moment, "Yes I do."

Damon chuckled as I took his clammy hand, "I always knew your love for my son would be your downfall."

I didn't comment, biting my tongue as he directed me to stand in between him and Malik. My mind and body screamed, sweat dripping down my spine as they circled around me. I was their prey. I had been since I had ascended at twenty-five. For three years my fear of them kept me away from Sihr, from my family, from the coven that I loved.

"Call on your magic." Malik directed.

I took a deep breath, closing my eyes as I imagined my magic outside of my body. Imagined that twisting ball of shadows that had been with me my entire life ripping from my chest to hang in the air in front of me. Wind suddenly began to pick up, causing my hair to fly out of the scarf I'd tied it into. "Very good, Larissa. Now repeat after us." Damon's voice yelled over the wind. "I give my power to you."

I gritted my teeth, "I give my power to you."

They both inhaled deeply, and I flinched as both of their hands landed on my shoulders, gripping me hard, "I release the gift given to me by the Mother and Father."

My tongue grew heavy in my mouth, but I repeated, "I release the gift given to me by the Mother and Father."

Suddenly the world around us went silent. I popped my eyes open to find Damon standing before me, mouth opened in a silent scream as blood poured down the front of his shirt. Over his shoulder I made eye contact with Sihr. A nod was all I needed. I twirled, yanking my magic back into my body, shadows rushing along my skin. Without a thought they wrapped around my fingers, solidifying into sharp talons as I wrapped my hand around Malik's throat. Strength that I didn't know I possessed had him dangling above the ground.

A voice that did not belong to me spoke from my lips, "You have spat in the face of your gods. Long have we watched your crimes, and long have we waited for this moment."

Chills ran down my spine as shadows rushed into every orifice of Malik's face. He gurgled and fought against my hold as shadows ripped him apart from the inside. It wasn't long before I was dropping my arm, allowing the shell of Malik's dead body to drop to the ground at my feet. I whirled around, searching for Sihr. He stood a few feet away, a tear rolling down his face as he looked down at his father's body.

"Are you okay?" I croaked, wrapping my arms around his middle.

"It's over." He said, pressing his lips to my forehead, "We are finally free."

"Should we leave--" I started to ask, but I watched in amazement as black flames consumed the bodies of the former Priests, "We need to give extra thanks at our next coven meeting."

"The Mother and Father have blessed us once again." Sihr said, holding my hand as we walked slowly out of the clearing. I could feel the weight lifting from my shoulders the further we got away.

Ten

Alok healed, though it took weeks for him to regain his strength. Malik and Damon had siphoned some magic away from him. His power would never be as strong as it was before, but none of us cared. He was alive and more than capable of filling his role as Priest.

Bambi and Fang stayed with us for a few days, ensuring that we were safe and able to handle our coven alone. Saying goodbye to my best friend was bittersweet. Of course, we both now had our witch bonds and covens to care for, but the bond of our sisterhood was strong. We would visit whenever time allowed, but we both knew it wouldn't be as often as we'd like. Thank the Mother and Father for cellphones. We FaceTimed at least once a week, gossiping about everything under the sun.

"Larissa, someone is here to see you," Alok called from downstairs.

I crawled off the bed, taking in the bright sunny day outside. We had upgraded to a larger bed so that we could all sleep together at night. It didn't hurt that it gave us more room for all the best positions. I had never been so well loved in my entire life. Sihr and Alok worked like a team in every way. My perfect shadow daddies. Just thinking of the way they had worked my body the night before had my thighs clenching together as I slipped into a long flowy dress. I made my way down the stairs, taking in the shadows that lazed around our home like pets now. With all of our power combined the coven had already seen huge increases in their reserves. All the rituals we'd performed had gone well.

"Larissa De Valois, you look radiant." A voice I hadn't heard since I was a teenager echoed out.

"Xava Dovey, what the hell are you doing here?" I shouted, rushing down the last few stairs and throwing my hands around the red head. I hadn't seen Xava in years. She'd spent two years with the Shadow coven for her Hex Guard training. Just before my mother died, Damon and Malik had sent her away. I'd receive a few letters from her over the years, but she had been mostly a ghost.

"Decided to stop off on my way to a job." She responded, "A little birdie told me you went and got bonds and became a Priestess."

I grinned, "Oh I'm sure I know the nosey little birdie that did that. It's so good to see you. How long will you be in town?"

"Just today. I've got to be up in Georgia for this job by Monday." Xava explained. She was an assassin for the Hex Guard. Of course, that wasn't her official job title, but I knew what she did.

"If you're heading to Georgia you should stop by the Blood Coven. My best friend, Bambi Cruor would love you." I said, "What's up? Where have you been the last few years."

A strain behind her eyes told me all that I needed to know, but she smiled anyway, "Here and there. You know how this line of work is. I just came back from Mexico."

"Tell me everything." I said, leading her to sit down.

Xava and I talked for hours, but as soon as the clock chimed six, she stood taking her leave. I was sad to see my friend leave so quickly, but I understood in her line of work that she didn't get to decide when or where she went. I couldn't imagine living like that, but she was a Protection witch. That was part of her power.

"Do I finally get to claim you again?" Sihr said as I entered the dining room.

"Xava is gone." I confirmed, taking a seat next to him. The staff had already laid out food for us, so I didn't hesitate to dig in. Alok would eat when he returned from his patrol.

"Perfect." He grinned. I wasn't sure what he was planning, but I didn't care as long as I got to eat dinner first.

An hour later, Alok strode into the room, taking in our empty plates with a sad sigh, "I missed dinner again?"

"You're just in time for dessert." Sihr smirked.

Alok and Sihr stared at each other for a moment before they turned to me. "Take off your dress." Alok commanded.

"Then get on your knees." Sihr added.

I glanced around the dining room for a moment, nervously, "Here?"

"She isn't doing as she's told." Sihr grunted.

"We'll have to punish her." Alok said, taking several long strides before he was before me. He grabbed the neck of my dress and tore it open. It fluttered to the ground around me. Before I could move, Alok had me pushed over the dining room table, "When your daddies tell you to do something you do it immediately. Do you understand?"

"Yes daddy." I said, pushing my ass out. The first slap was a shock straight through my core. Sihr moved around me, and then they were both raining slaps down on my ass. Heat built on my skin, pain mixing with pleasure as their unrelenting strikes roved lower. My legs were kicked apart; fingers ran over my pussy. I moaned, but it was cut off by a sharp slap between my legs. I yelped, nearly standing up, but a firm hand on my neck kept me in position.

"This is a punishment, ombra." Sihr growled, "You're not supposed to enjoy it." A second slap to my pussy had a tear running down my face. A couple more and I was begging them to do something, anything. I was on fire and only their cocks could put me out.

"Do you think she's had enough?" Alok asked, running his hands over my sore ass.

A finger pressed into my pussy, "She's good and ready for us." Sihr responded.

"On the table, on your knees." Alok commanded, and I scrambled up, arching my back and pressing my cheek against the cool surface, "So good and responsive. Just a little punishment and she'll be the perfect good girl for us."

"I am going to take her mouth." Sihr growled, coming in front of me. His cock bobbed in my line of vision, and I opened my mouth. He slapped himself across my cheek twice, before plunging down my throat. I wasn't prepared for Alok to slam into my pussy at the same time, causing me to splutter and cough around the cock blocking my airway.

They fucked in perfect rhythm, rocking me back and forth between them until I had no idea where I began and they ended. A cool feeling against my ass was the only preparation I got before a shadow pressed into my ass. "All of your holes should be filled all the time, my dark angel." Alok growled.

Faster and harder they took me until I was crying out with the most powerful orgasm of my life. The world stopped as I came, wave after wave of pleasurable pain washing over me. My mouth and pussy were flooded with cum simultaneously as my men also found their release. When we all came down. Alok gathered me up, carrying me to our bed. The moment he laid me down, Sihr was there, wiping every inch of me clean.

I had never felt more loved and cared for than I did as they curled around me pressing kisses and affirmations into my skin. Instead of my coven feeling like a burden, it had been my freedom. Shadows curled around us, blanketing the room in a comforting darkness as we drifted off to sleep.

Epilogue

Sihr

L arissa's giggle as she crouched in the small closet was music to my ears. It was rare to see her so carefree. My Priestess was always to be taken seriously. I guess that's how she had conned me into playing this game with her. To be fair, any chance to see Alok shaken was plenty of reward for me. I cared for him like a brother, but sometimes he needed to be reminded of his place. "Hush, he's going to hear you." I whispered into her ear, unable to keep my hands from roaming over her slim hips.

It was too dark in here to see her eyes, but the slight hitching of her breath told me I was having the same effect on her that she was having on me. "Save it for Alok, ombra."

Locked in the dark with my bond had been my dream six months ago. I still couldn't believe that the Mother and Father had given Larissa's two bonds, but I couldn't be more thankful that I got to stand by her side. The coven was thriving under her steady guidance, their adoration of the tiny Priestess growing every day.

"Rissa? Sihr? Where are you?" Alok's voice filled the small space as Larissa buzzed with excitement. We both held our breath as he approached our shared bed. The small slats in the closet door didn't give us the best view as he sat down, only to be grabbed by shadows and yanked until he was spread eagle on the bed.

Larissa burst from the closet, "It's my turn, big man."

Alok glanced to me for help, but I shrugged, "If it's Ris or you, I'm on her side every time."

Larissa crawled onto the bed, straddling his chest, "You thought I'd forget it's your birthday, didn't you?"

"Are you my present?" He asked. I could see him struggling against the shadows holding him, but Larissa's magic was too strong for him to easily break.

"Something like that." She purred. She stood on the bed, pulling the thin dress she'd been wearing over her head. Her body was sleek, muscular yet luscious in all the right places. Standing over Alok made her seem even smaller if that was possible. His almost seven-foot frame usually dwarfed her, but instead he was prostrated before her like the goddess that she was. I forced myself to sit in the chair in the corner. I would only watch the show tonight. That was its own form of torture, but I would do almost anything Larissa asked of me. "I think you've been a very bad boy." Her words brought my attention back to the scene before me.

Alok whimpered as she ran her hand over his hard cock, "Mommy, you wouldn't punish me on my birthday, would you?"

Something about that title aroused Larissa, I could see the way her thighs clinched at his words. "Payback is a bitch." She whispered before all of the clothes on his body shredded away. Her nails left small tracks of blood over his chest as she slowly made her way closer to Alok's cock. The way her pussy rubbed along him was obscene, and I couldn't help but palm my own cock as it responded to seeing them together. She teased his cock against her entrance for a long time, his moans filled the room, but she kept him under control with a single look. Larissa had always been that way. While she loved for us to use and control her body, she could just as easily control us.

Finally, she sank down onto his cock, setting what I knew was a torturous space as she ran her hands over his chest. He groaned when she tweaked his nipples, and I wondered if I would enjoy the same treatment. "Can you be a good boy and make me cum with just your cock?" Larissa moaned as she bounced faster.

Alok growled, pushing past just a bit of Larissa's magic so that he could slam his hips into hers. She leaned forward, seeking her teeth into his already abused chest. Shadows curled around her hips, and I knew Alok had more control than she'd planned. Watching as the two of them fucked fast and hard was enough for me to stand, cock in hand as I climbed on the bed, "Take me in your mouth, ombra. Show our bond just how well you can take me." She grinned up at me, melting my heart just a bit before her warm mouth enveloped me. She sucked me greedily, taking me until I was pressed into the back of her throat. The tears in her eyes sent me over the edge. She swallowed every drop of cum down, before pressing a soft kiss to my stomach, and returning her attention to Alok. "I still haven't cum. Do I need to punish you more?" She moved off his cock, crawling until she straddled his face, "If you don't make me cum, I'm going to leave you tied up here for the rest of the night. Sihr and I will go enjoy the amazing dinner we made." We had spent the first several hours of our day prepping Alok's favorite dishes from lemon glazed salmon to Gramma's famous gumbo.

Alok was quick with his tongue, Larissa's moans a symphony as I dressed and pulled out new clothes for them. When I stepped back out into the room I was greeted with the sight of Larissa's hand wrapped around Alok's throat as she rode him hard. She chanted, "Cum for me." Until finally he roared his orgasm, their bodies shuttering together from the force. All the shadows disappeared a few moments later, Alok carefully lifting Larissa from his lap as he stood.

"That was fun." He grinned, taking the clothes from my arms, "Baby, if payback is a bitch just wait until you see what I have in store for you."

Larissa groaned, "Y'all will be the death of me."

I kissed her head as I passed, "La petite mort won't kill you, ombra."

The sounds of her laughter chased me down the staircase. The Shadow Coven was finally starting to heal. I was healing, and it was all because of Larissa. Without her power we would never have defeated my father. Without her I would never have climbed out of the blackhole of disappear I'd lived in when she'd run away. Before I stepped into the kitchen I muttered a quiet prayer, "Thank you, Mother and Father. I won't ever forget what you've blessed me with."

Acknowledgements

Two Shadowed Hearts was one of my favorite stories to write. It appeared in my head, fully fleshed out when the character of Larissa appeared on page in One Bloody Night. I knew her story had to be told. The first person I have to shout out here is my lovely artist, Larissa. She gave me her permission to use her name for a character when no other name seemed to fit. The fact that she draws all of my characters (and does my tattoos!) made this very sweet. Thank you so much for your support, girl! It means the world every time you bring one of my visions to life.

As always, my family and my fiancé do everything they can to keep me going when being an author and a full-time person gets to be too much. With their unending support I continue to get to live my dreams every day. There is no end to their love and patience with me. I will never be able to repay their efforts on my behalf.

Leah, my amazing cover artist, PA, and best friend... There really aren't enough words to acknowledge how much you have improved my journey as an author. Every cover you make and stress you take off my plate means the world. I can't wait for them to read the next book.

To my street team, you lovely ladies make my author world go round. Without your help in getting the word out about my books I have no doubt I would never have gotten this far.

And finally, to you. Yes you. Every page that you decide to read makes a difference to me as the author. Your support and desire to see more of my work keeps me going when I want to give up. I hope you enjoyed Larissa, Alok, and Sihr. I promise you'll be seeing more of them in future books.

Also by

The Reclaiming Wonderland Series
Code Red
Code White: Frosted Wonderland (Coming December 2025)
Blue Dreams
Emerald Knights (Coming Spring 2026)

The Austral Witches
Primal Echoes (Coming September 2025)
One Bloody Night
Two Shadowed Hearts
Three Little Doves (Coming February 2026)

About the author

Taila has always had an obsession with stories, cultivated by a loving grandmother. She always had her nose in some book or another, but at fourteen she began writing her own stories. Code Red may be the first to publication, but you can expect many, many more to come. Taila lives in the hills of East Tennessee. Where she can often be found cuddling naughty kittens, reading, or working her day job. Occasionally, her family or partner will convince her to leave her cave to see the outside world.

If you want to chat with Taila or stalk the socials for book updates:

Facebook Page: Taila Cantrell Author

Facebook Group: Taila Cantrell's Cuties

Instagram: tcantrellauthor

TikTok: @tailatalks